AP ''22

BURNHAM MEMORIAL LIBRARY
COLCHESTER   05446

DISCARDED

W9-ATS-507

Little Mouse Adventures

MINDFULNESS AT THE PARK

Little Mouse Adventures: Mindfulness at the Park
Copyright © 2020 by Teresa Anne Power

All rights reserved. No part of this book may be used or reproduced in any manner whatsoever without written permission except in the case of brief quotations embodied in critical articles and reviews.

For information, address:
Stafford House Books, Inc.
P.O. Box 291, Pacific Palisades, CA 90272
www.staffordhousebooks.com

The author and publisher of this book disclaim any liability in connection with the exercises and advice contained herein.

Library of Congress Control Number: 2020930262
ISBN: 978-1-7344786-0-0 Hardback
ISBN: 978-1-7344786-1-7 Ebook

Editing: Author Bridge Media, www.AuthorBridgeMedia.com
Book Design: Najdan Mancic, Iskon Design, www.iskonbookdesign.com
Illustrations by Emma Allen

This book is dedicated to my father, who was an avid supporter of me and my vision of spreading yoga around the world with my books and also Kids' Yoga Day.

printed in China

Little Mouse Adventures

MINDFULNESS AT THE PARK

written by
TERESA ANNE POWER

illustrated by
EMMA ALLEN

STAFFORD HOUSE BOOKS

Little Mouse loves playing games with
his best friend, Mr. Opus. They play near
the cozy burrow where Little Mouse's
family lives, under an old oak tree.

In the afternoons, Little Mouse visits Mr. Opus at his house, where Tammy McDoodle and her parents live.

Tammy and her mom enjoy
doing yoga together. Little Mouse
and Mr. Opus like to follow along
as best they can.

The flamingo pose is Little Mouse's favorite. It reminds him of his friend, Rosita, from the zoo. When Little Mouse stretches like a flamingo, he feels calm.

One day,
Tammy's mom
tells her about
something called
mindfulness.

"When you are quiet and pay attention to your breath," says Tammy's mom, "you can stay calm and focused, no matter what is going on around you. That's called mindfulness."

One Saturday, Tammy's mom and dad plan a trip to a nearby park. Tammy is so excited that she rushes through breakfast so they can leave right away.

"Try to focus on your breath to stay calm," Mr.
Opus says to Little Mouse.
"I'm too excited to be calm!" says Little Mouse.

At the park, Little Mouse enjoys the gentle wind and sweet smell of grass. Mr. Opus strolls slowly along the path. Tammy skips as she breathes in the fresh air.

"Think of yourself as a mighty and solid tree," says Tammy's mom as she and Tammy hold the tree pose.

"Breathe deeply in and out of your nose."

"Sometimes we have too many thoughts in our heads," says Tammy's mom.

"Focusing on our breath helps to calm those thoughts and enjoy the world around us."

"Here's another way to calm your mind," says Tammy's mom. "Take a deep breath through your nose, count to five, then breathe out slowly."

Tammy slowly counts her breaths while breathing in and out.

"One. Two. Three. Four. Five." She feels a sense of calm come over her.

Breathing quietly reminds Mr.
Opus of child's pose. Little Mouse
feels like he's floating on a cloud.

Little Mouse still has his eyes closed as the McDoodle family and Mr. Opus get up and continue their walk in the park.

Little Mouse opens his eyes in surprise when he hears a dog barking. He gets scared when he doesn't see the McDoodle family or Mr. Opus.

As the dog comes closer, Little
Mouse is afraid. His mind races, and
he does not know what to do.

Then Little Mouse remembers the words of
Tammy's mom and Mr. Opus.

"Breathe deeply," Little Mouse says to himself.
"Stay calm."

He breathes in and out as he counts,
"One. Two. Three. Four. Five."

When the dog comes closer to Little Mouse, it stops barking and slowly breathes in and out. "Do you know about mindful breathing too?" asks Little Mouse.

"Of course," says the dog.

"I was scared because I lost my owner. I was barking because I was afraid. But watching you reminded me to stay quiet and calm."

"I'm sorry that you are lost. I'm Little Mouse."

"Hello," says the dog. "I'm Sparky."

Mr. Opus returns to find Little Mouse. "This is Sparky," says Little Mouse.

"Very nice to meet you," say Mr. Opus and Sparky to each other.

Little Mouse and Mr. Opus catch up with Tammy and her parents. As they prepare to go home, Little Mouse sees Sparky running towards a relieved looking man.

"Goodbye, Sparky," says Little Mouse, waving to the dog. "I'm so glad you found your owner."

Hilly Park
Opening Times
Monday - 6-8
Tuesday - 6-8
Wednesday - 6-8
Thursday - 6-8
Friday - 6-8
Saturday - 6-10
Sunday - 7-6

Back home, Tammy tries to quiet her
mind when she feels overly excited or anxious.
Breathing deeply makes her feel calmer around
her family and friends.

Back in his burrow, Little Mouse shares with his family what he has learned.

That night, just before he goes to bed,
Little Mouse practices quieting his mind
before peacefully drifting off to sleep. He
can't wait to have more adventures!

BURNHAM MEMORIAL LIBRARY
COLCHESTER, VT. 05446

DISCARDED